Meet Buckley!

A story about my dog,
in both Hindi and English

Story written by: Neha Shah
Illustrations: Mousam Bannerjee

Inspired by my dog Buckley.

Inspired for my nieces, nephews, and all curious kids around the world.

Meet Buckley!

Buckley Sey Millo!

Buckley lives in Austin.
Buckley Austin may rayhta hay.

Austin is a city in Texas.
Austin ka shahar Texas may hay.

Buckley likes to go to the park.
Buckley ko park jaana pasund hay.

Buckley brings his red ball to the park.
Buckley apni laal gaind park le jaata hay.

Buckley runs in the park.
Buckley park may bhaaghta hay.

Buckley runs the fastest in the park.
Buckley park may sabsay tez bhaaghta hay.

Every morning, Buckley and his mom go running.

Har subaah, Buckley aur uski mummy bhaagnay jaahtay heyy.

Buckley likes to run outside.

Buckley ko baahar bhaagna pasund hay.

Sometimes Buckley stops.
Kabhi kabhi, Buckley rukta hay.

Buckley smells the flowers.
Buckley phoolow ko soongta hay.

He says 'hi' to the butterflies.
Woh tithleeyo ko 'hi' bolta hay.

In the afternoon, Buckley and his dad go to the coffee shop.
Doepayhar may, Buckley aur uskay papa coffee ki dukan jaatay heyy.

The people at the coffee shop are very nice.
Coffee ki dukan kay lowgh bahut ahchay heyy.

They give Buckley snacks.
Woh Buckley ko khaana daytay heyy.

Today, **Buckley** is sitting **in the** car.
Aaj, **Buckley** gaadi **may** beytha **hay.**

Where is **Buckley** going?
Buckley kahaa jaa raha **hay?**

Is Buckley going to the coffee shop?
Keya Buckley coffee ki dukan jah raha hay?

No, he is not going there.
Naahi, woh wahaa naahi jaa raha hay.

Is Buckley going to the park?

Keya Buckley park jaa raha hay?

No, he is not going to the park.

Nahi, woh park nahi jaa raha hay.

Buckley is upset.
Buckley dookhi hay.

"Where are we going?", Buckley wonders.
"Hum kaha jah rahay heyy?", Buckley soachta hay.

Buckley is tired.
Buckley thakaa hai.

Buckley sleeps in the car.
Buckley gaadi may sota hai.

The car stops. Buckley wakes up.
Gaadi rukti hay. Buckley oothta hay.

WOW! Buckley is at his grandma's house!
Waah! Buckley apni dadi kay ghar pay hay!

Buckley is very happy!
Buckley bahot khush hay!

Buckley is with his family.
Buckley apnay parivaar kay saath hay.

Buckley loves his family very much!
Buckley apnay parivaar ko bahut pyaar karta hay!

Made in the USA
Lexington, KY
17 December 2019